WATERSHIP™ DOWN

Bigwig Learns a Lesson

Diane Redmond

RED FOX

A Red Fox Book

Published by Random House Children's Books
20 Vauxhall Bridge Road, London SW1V 2SA

A division of The Random House Group Ltd
London Melbourne Sydney Auckland
Johannesburg and agencies throughout the world

www.watershipdown.net

Illustrations by County Studio, Leicester

1   3   5   7   9   10   8   6   4   2

Printed and bound in Italy by Lego SPA

THE RANDOM HOUSE GROUP Limited Reg. No. 954009

www.randomhouse.co.uk

ISBN 0 09 940335 8

This story represents scenes from the television series, Watership Down,
which is inspired by Richard Adams' novel of the same name.

The rabbits were settling in on
Watership Down, when one dark night, Holly
arrived. He was scratched and dirty, and looked
very different from the Holly they had known before.
'Fiver's dream was right,' he said. 'Our warren *was*
destroyed. Pimpernel escaped with me.'
He hung his head. 'But we're all that's left.'
'Don't worry,' said Bigwig. 'You're safe now.'

The next morning, Holly was feeling much better. 'I want to go and look for Pimpernel,' he said. 'I left him in a fine big warren that's quite close by.'

Bigwig looked excited. 'A fine warren, you say, I like the idea of that!'

Fiver blinked in surprise. 'What? Surely you'd never leave Watership Down.'

Bigwig nodded. 'It's not much fun up here without a burrow.'

'Well, I don't see why we can't go and look,' said Hazel. 'I'll tell the others.'

Under the beech tree, earth was flying everywhere. Blackberry was halfway down a hole, digging. The other rabbits were eating.

Hazel ran up. 'We're off to find Pimpernel,' he said.

'Good idea!' said Dandelion. 'Can we come, too?'

'It's just Bigwig, Fiver and me this time,' said Hazel. 'Blackberry needs your help here.' And before his friends could argue, he ran off down the slope.

Holly led the rabbits down the hill and through some woods to a clearing, where two fat rabbits were grazing.

'That's Cowslip and Strawberry,' said Holly.

'They look very calm, for rabbits,' said Bigwig.

'Look at those huge burrows!' cried Hazel. 'We'd never build a warren like that – it's far too open.'

'I don't think I like this,' said Fiver. 'It feels bad.'

Bigwig laughed. 'You're always worried, Fiver! It looks very comfortable to me.'

When the fat rabbits saw they had visitors, they rose up onto their back legs and started to dance a slow, strange dance.

'Welcome, welcome. Greetings all!' they sang. 'So very nice of you to call!'

'What's wrong with them?' Hazel whispered to Holly. 'I've never seen rabbits do that before.'

Holly shrugged. 'It's how they greet visitors,' he whispered back. He turned to Cowslip. 'We've come for Pimpernel. Have you seen him?'

But Cowslip ignored his question. 'It's starting to rain,' he said instead. 'Why don't you come inside?'

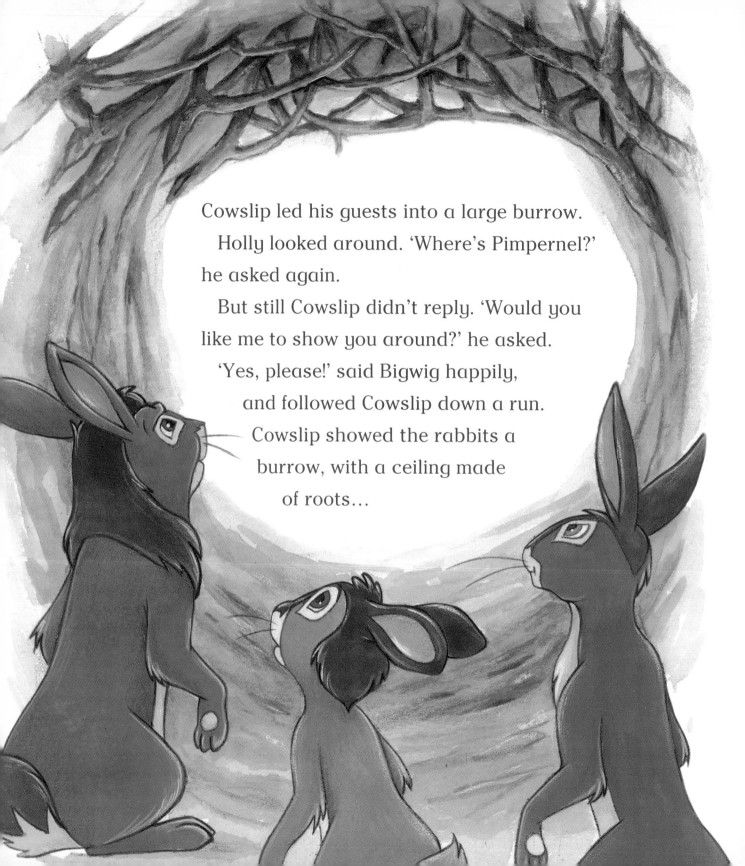

Cowslip led his guests into a large burrow.

Holly looked around. 'Where's Pimpernel?'
he asked again.

But still Cowslip didn't reply. 'Would you
like me to show you around?' he asked.

'Yes, please!' said Bigwig happily,
and followed Cowslip down a run.

Cowslip showed the rabbits a
burrow, with a ceiling made
of roots…

…and another that had stones and pieces of glass pressed into the wall.

'What's this?' asked Hazel.

Strawberry laughed. 'It's a shape. We made it.'

Fiver trembled. What kind of rabbits made patterns on their walls?

By evening, Bigwig had settled into Cowslip's warren like he
was one of the family.

'This is the life,' he said, tucking into some lettuce. 'A full
belly and a warm bed. What more could a rabbit want?'

But Fiver wasn't eating. He sat in a dark corner and watched.

After a while, he hopped over to Bigwig. 'This is a bad place,' he whispered. 'We must leave!'

'What, now?' cried Bigwig. 'In the rain? Don't be silly.'

'There's terrible danger here!' cried Fiver. 'It's safer outside with the foxes!' And he fled from the burrow.

The next morning Hazel found Fiver sitting outside. 'What's the matter?' he asked.

'Someone had to stand watch,' said Fiver. 'There's evil all around us. Please, Hazel, let's go home.'

Bigwig called from the entrance of the burrow. 'Hazel, we're off to get food!'

'Come with us, Fiver,' said Hazel.

Fiver started trembling. 'No, it's wrong,' he said. 'The food, this place, those rabbits…'

Bigwig bounded over. 'Is Fiver still moaning?' he asked. 'Well I like it here. In fact, I think I'm going to stay.' And the big rabbit hopped away.

Suddenly a scream filled the air. Hazel raced towards the cries and found Bigwig lying on his side. A silver wire was tight around his neck.

'Help!' Hazel called. 'Bigwig's caught in a trap!'

Fiver rushed across and tried to bite through the wire, but the metal was too hard.

Holly ran to the warren. He asked the fat rabbits for help, but they just stared at the ground.

Cowslip looked at him. 'There is no Bigwig. There never was,' he said.

'You're mad!' cried Holly. 'All of you!' Then he turned and ran.

Hazel was examining the wire. 'Look, Fiver,' he said. 'It's attached to a peg that's stuck in the ground. We can dig it out – like a carrot!'

The rabbits started to dig. When the hole was big enough, Fiver dived down and nibbled the peg until it split in half.

'You're free, Bigwig,' whispered Hazel. 'Come on, get up.'

But the big rabbit's eyes were closed and he lay still.

Strawberry crept up. 'The man will come soon and take him away,' he said. 'Like he did with Pimpernel.'

The rabbits looked shocked.

'What are you saying?' said Holly.

'The man feeds us and protects us,' said Strawberry. 'Then he catches us in his traps. Until that happens, we have an easy time.'

'But that's no life for a rabbit!' said Hazel.

Suddenly, Bigwig moved. 'Ow, my neck hurts,' he groaned.

'You're all right!' said Hazel.

'Yes,' gasped Bigwig. 'But you were right, Fiver, this place isn't. Let's go.'

'Take me with you!' begged Strawberry. 'I don't want to stay here.'

'No,' snarled Bigwig. 'You lied to us.'

Hazel looked at the sad rabbit. 'Yes, come with us,' he said. 'But I warn you, we live a hard life up in the hills.'

The rabbits turned, scampered back through the woods and climbed the long steep hill up to Watership Down. At the top, Hawkbit, Pipkin and Dandelion appeared, covered in dirt and mud.

'I hope you've had a nice time roaming around the countryside while we've been digging!' said Hawkbit.

Bigwig smiled at Hazel. 'Home, sweet home,' he laughed.